Are you brave enough
to come into
the Wilderness?

The moment you step across
the boundary,
you'll be changed forever . . .

The Wilderness

N
W   E
S

Ogre Tree

Lake of the Dead

Forest of Forever Night

River Camp

Holloway

Green Slime River

Drawbridge

Willow's Garden

???

Witch's
Hut

Dragon
Gardens

Valley of
Killer Plants

Swamp

Skull
Rock

Raven's
Garden

For Odette and Odile.—G.L.

For Matt. Again. Because he's the best and wildest
stick embellisher there ever was.—R.B.

OXFORD
UNIVERSITY PRESS

Great Clarendon Street, Oxford OX2 6DP
Oxford University Press is a department of the University of Oxford.
It furthers the University's objective of excellence in research, scholarship,
and education by publishing worldwide. Oxford is a registered trade mark
of Oxford University Press in the UK and in certain other countries

Text copyright © Gill Lewis 2021
Illustrations copyright © Rebecca Bagley 2021

The moral rights of the author have been asserted

Database right Oxford University Press (maker)

First published 2021

British Library Cataloguing in Publication Data

Data available

ISBN: 978-0-19-277177-3

1 3 5 7 9 10 8 6 4 2

Printed in China

Paper used in the production of this book is a natural,
recyclable product made from wood grown in sustainable forests.
The manufacturing process conforms to the environmental
regulations of the country of origin.

Willow Wildthing
and the
Shooting Star

Written by Gill Lewis

Illustrated by Rebecca Bagley

OXFORD
UNIVERSITY PRESS

Chapter 1
Dark Clouds

Willow stared out of her bedroom window and wished it would stop raining.

It had rained for days.

Rained . . .

and rained . . .

and rained.

It hadn't stopped.

Water poured from the gutters and streamed down the windows.

Big wide pools spread across the garden.

It wasn't yet evening, but even the street lights had lit up. They glowed orange against the dark sky.

Far in the distance, thunder rumbled.

Willow shivered and stared out at the black clouds.

It felt as if the whole sky was pressing down on her.

Everything was going wrong.

Clouds were like worries, she thought. They got bigger and bigger, and darker and darker, until they burst, and all the troubles came pouring out.

Willow's little three-year-old brother Freddie was ill again, and Willow thought it was all her fault. Freddie hadn't been well since birth and sometimes needed time in hospital. He had to be careful not to pick up infections, but Willow had come home from school with a cold and passed it on to Freddie. Now Freddie had the cold too, and he was coughing and coughing and couldn't stop. Mum and Dad were packing things together to take him back to the hospital.

'It's not your fault,' said Mum. 'He could have picked up a cold from anyone. These things just happen.'

Willow turned to see Mum standing in the doorway with Freddie's hospital bag in her arms.

'Nana will be here soon,' said Mum. 'She's looking forward to coming and babysitting you.'

'I'm not a baby, Mum,' said Willow.

Mum sighed. 'You know what I mean. I don't know what time Dad and I will get back from the hospital. We may need to stay there overnight.'

'I want to come with you,' said Willow.

'Sorry, love. You know you can't this time,' said Mum. 'The doctors have asked people who have colds to stay away from other patients. Besides, Nana will love to see you.'

'It's fine,' said Willow. But it wasn't fine. She had to stay home with Nana. Willow loved seeing Nana, but Nana worried about her too much and never let Willow out of her sight. She wouldn't even let Willow take Sniff for a walk on their own around the block.

'Uff!' barked Sniff, as if he knew what she was thinking.

Sniff was Willow's dog. No one had

wanted him at the rescue centre. He was a small scruffy dog with one eye and wonky teeth, but the moment Willow saw him, she just knew they had to be together.

'Can you sit with Freddie until we're ready to go?' said Mum.

Willow went downstairs and sat beside Freddie on the sofa. Sniff jumped up too and wedged himself between them.

Freddie was coughing and trying to suck his thumb at the same time. He felt hot and was cross and grizzly.

Willow put her arm around him and stroked his forehead.

Freddie pressed his head into her shoulder and looked up at her. 'Story?' he asked.

Freddie loved listening to Willow's made-up stories, but right now she couldn't even think of one to tell. She looked out of the window again at the scrubby patch of woodland beyond the garden. The trees were veiled in rain, and it looked like a small tropical jungle in the middle of the town. The scrubby woodland had been the gardens and grounds of an old house that had burned down long ago. Houses and roads had been built up all around it, and now it was a wasteland that adults said needed tidying. But it was a wasteland that held a secret. It hid a wilderness inside that Willow and her friends explored. It was a wild place in the middle of the town where they had adventures.

'Story?' said Freddie again.

'Once upon a time . . .' began Willow, but she couldn't think of a thing to say. The hammering of raindrops became louder and louder until she couldn't think at all.

She wished it would stop raining. She wished Freddie was not ill and she wished she could go and see her friends, the Wild Things, in the Wilderness again.

If Nana came, the Wilderness and the Wild Things would have to wait.

Sniff whined in agreement. Then his ears pricked up and jumped out of her arms. 'Uff, uff, uff!'

Someone was rapping urgently on the front door.

That'll be Nana, thought Willow.

But it wasn't Nana.

'Willow!' Dad called. 'Someone to see you.'

Willow lifted Freddie up in her arms and carried him to the door. There was a girl a bit older than Willow standing on the mat, with water dripping from her long black cloak.

'Raven!' said Willow. 'What are you doing here?'

Raven was one of the friends she went to the Wilderness with. She was one of

the Wild Things she had met and shared adventures with. When they were in the Wilderness, Raven seemed more like a bird than a girl, but here, standing on the mat, she looked oddly normal. Wet too.

Sniff barked and jumped up and down trying to lick Raven's hands.

'You've got to come to the Wilderness,' whispered Raven.

'Willow glanced back at Mum and Dad in the kitchen. 'I can't.'

'You have to,' said Raven.

Willow could see Raven was close to tears. 'What is it?' She had a feeling that the day was going from bad to worse.

'It's River Camp,' said Raven. 'The floodwater is rising. It's going to go under water.'

Willow thought of their camp nestled in the bend of the river. It was their special den made from branches and an old tarpaulin. They had rugs and cushions inside. She thought of the campfire where they made hot chocolate and toasted marshmallows. It was where they read books, drew maps, and planned adventures. It was their safe, secret place, away from the outside world. She tried not to imagine the swirling dark water taking all those things away.

'You have to come,' insisted Raven. 'We're going to lose everything.'

Chapter 2
Sky Elephants

'I can't,' said Willow. 'Mum and Dad are taking Freddie to the hospital, and Nana is on her way here. I know they won't let me out.'

Just then, the phone rang.

Dad answered it, and Willow could see a frown form on his face.

'That was Nana,' said Dad. He shook his head. 'She can't get here because a road near her house has flooded.'

Mum tutted and looked at the clock. 'What are we going to do? One of us will have to stay with Willow.'

Willow could feel tears form. She felt in the way again. She felt it was her fault that Mum and Dad couldn't both go to the hospital. She felt it was her fault Freddie was ill.

'Willow can stay with me,' said Raven.

Mum and Dad looked at Raven. They had been rushing about so much that they hadn't really noticed her.

'I live at the end house,' she said.

Willow looked at her mum. 'Can I? Please?'

Willow's mum frowned. 'I don't know. It's a bit sudden. What will your parents say?'

Raven smiled. 'Mum will be fine with it. Sniff can come too. My mum loves dogs. She used to have one, but we can't get another because she's at work all day.'

'Well, if you're sure,' said Mum. 'It would be a huge help.'

'I'll get my stuff,' said Willow. She passed Freddie to her mum and rushed upstairs to pack spare clothes and a toothbrush. Then she grabbed her raincoat and welly boots from the porch. Sniff bounced around her, certain that this was the beginning of an adventure.

Mum and Dad were already putting Freddie in the car. He was sitting in his car seat with his arms outstretched to Willow, calling her name.

Willow leaned into the car. 'I can't come

this time. I'm not allowed.'

'Story?' said Freddie.

Willow reached over and gave him a hug.
'I'll find one for you and tell you when you
come home,' she said. 'I promise.'

She shut the car door and pressed her
face against the glass, poking her tongue out
and making him smile. She turned to Mum.
'He will be OK?'

Mum nodded, but Willow could see she
looked worried. 'He'll be fine,' said Mum.
'He just needs a bit of extra care at the
moment.' She gave Willow a big hug. 'The
question is, will you be OK?'

Willow nodded, although she didn't
feel OK. She felt helpless. She wanted to
be with Freddie. She didn't want to upset
Mum, so she pretended to be brave instead.

'I'll be fine.'

Mum zipped up Willow's coat. 'We'll let
you know how Freddie is. Now, off you go.
You and Raven will get soaked standing out
here. Dad and I need to go too.'

Willow walked with Raven along the wet
pavement to Raven's house. Mum and Dad's
car passed them, and Willow felt an ache of
sadness. She felt left behind, again.

'Uff!' barked Sniff, running ahead of them.

Willow smiled. She still had Sniff, and
right now Sniff was excited about this new
adventure.

'This is my house,' said Raven. 'We'll
dump your stuff and go and meet the other
Wild Things in the Wilderness.'

Willow had never been to Raven's house
before. She had only met Raven in the

Wilderness. Her house smelled of spice and incense. It was strange how everyone's houses smelled different.

'Hi Mum!' yelled Raven. 'Is it OK if Willow and Sniff stay the night?'

Raven's mum was in the kitchen, drinking coffee. 'Yes, of course.' She bent down to Sniff and rubbed his ears.

'We're going out,' said Raven.

Raven's mum looked outside. 'It's a bit wet.'

'We'll be fine. I've got my coat,' said Raven.

Raven's mum looked at Sniff. 'Well, Sniff hasn't got one.' She rummaged in the back of a cupboard and brought out an old dog coat. It was green with a reflective strip. 'This used to belong to Smartie, my old dog. It might fit Sniff.'

Willow pulled it on and it fitted perfectly.

'Come on,' said Raven. 'We have to go.'

Willow followed Raven out the back door and down Raven's garden to the path that ran along the back of all the gardens. The ditch between the path and the Wilderness was full of water. The Wild Things had named it the Green Slime River because it was full of weeds and algae. Strange things stirred and bubbled from its depths. It marked the boundary to the Wilderness, where time and distance stretched and where anything could happen. Willow and Raven crossed the plank. Usually they took off their shoes and ran barefoot through the Wilderness, but the ground was too cold and wet even for them.

Willow stood and looked around her. Despite the rain, she could feel the magic

of the Wilderness seep into her. Rain
pattered down through the leaves. The
wind rushing through the treetops roared
like an ocean from another world. Behind
her, lights from the houses glowed in
the gloom. She could see people inside,
in the dry and the warm. They seemed
far, far away somehow. She turned her
back on them and followed Raven into
the Wilderness. The only way in was

through the Holloway, a tunnel of thorns and brambles. Willow and Raven crawled on their hands and knees. By the time they reached the other side, they were soaked and covered in mud.

Willow stood beside Raven at the top of the slope and looked down into the valley. River Camp lay below them in the bend of the river, and there were four figures busily building a low wall of mud and branches around the camp.

Fox looked up at them. 'Come and help us!' he yelled. 'If we don't build this wall, River Camp will flood.'

Willow and Raven scrambled down the knotted roots of trees to join the other Wild Things.

Fox, Hare, Bear, and Mouse were completely covered in mud. Mouse was shivering with cold. Willow knelt down beside them and started packing more mud against the wall.

'The water is rising, and there is more rain coming,' said Hare, looking up at the dark clouds.

'I can't stop it coming through,' said Bear.

'We need more mud!' yelled Fox.

The Wild Things packed more mud against the walls, but as fast as they worked,

the rising waters ate away at the mud and loosened the sticks.

A flash of lightning tore through the sky.

Hare looked up and began counting. 'One elephant . . . two elephants . . . three elephants . . . four elephants . . . five elephants . . .'

Thunder rumbled in the clouds.

'What are you doing?' asked Willow.

Mouse put his finger against his lips. 'Shh! Hare is counting the sky elephants.'

'Sky elephants?' said Willow.

'Yes,' whispered Mouse. 'Can't you hear them up there?'

'I'm counting the seconds between the flash and the thunder,' said Hare. She turned to the Wild Things. 'The storm is a mile away.'

'We have to build the wall higher!' cried Fox.

Willow gathered armfuls of sticks to help hold the mud in place.

Another fork of lightning ripped the sky in a jagged neon line.

'One elephant . . . two elepha . . .' said Hare.

'BOOOOOOM! BUDDDABOOOOOM!' The thunder roared and rumbled.

'The sky elephants are coming!' yelled Mouse.

'The storm is almost here!' shouted Hare. 'We have to run.'

Chapter 3
Too Wet for Witches

'Let's go to the Dragon Gardens,' said Raven. 'We can shelter in the grotto.'

Fox looked around the camp. 'We're going to lose everything. We'll have to save what we can.'

The Wild Things gathered as much as they could. Hare grabbed her maps and her pens and pencils. Bear grabbed the tins of biscuits and hot chocolate. Willow helped Mouse pick up the cushions and

books before the floodwater reached them.
Raven pulled down the tarpaulin sheet
that covered the shelter and helped wrap
everything up inside it.

'Come on!' shouted Raven, leading the
way up the steep slope.

They scrambled and hauled the tarpaulin
up to the top of the slope in time to see a
surge of water burst the wall and swamp
River Camp completely.

An old leather suitcase bobbed on the
water and floated away to join the current of
the river.

'No!' yelled Fox. 'My telescope. It's in
there.' He began sliding down the slope.

'Come back!' shouted Raven.

But Fox was already wading through the
water.

27

Raven rushed after him, grabbed his arm, and pulled him up to higher ground. 'No! It's too dangerous. You'll be washed away too.'

Fox turned to watch the suitcase enter the fast water of the river. It tumbled over and over and disappeared from sight. He slumped down. 'My telescope was in that suitcase,' he said. 'My nan gave it to me before she died.'

A splintering sound rose up from the valley, and all the Wild Things looked to see the waters pull at the branches holding the camp together. The whole shelter came tumbling down. They watched as everything was washed away down the river.

'It's gone,' said Mouse. 'River Camp is gone.'

Willow put her arm around Mouse.

Hare buried her head in Raven's cloak, and Bear just stared at where their camp had once been. 'We got out just in time.'

Raven shook her head. 'Everything's gone. The whole Wilderness is flooded.'

Another flash lit the sky, and the sky elephants rampaged above.

'Come on,' called Fox. 'We need to get out of the storm.'

They followed Hare but stopped where the path ended in a vast lake. The water spread out before them. It looked dark and cold and was pitted with raindrops.

'The Great Swamp is flooded too,' said Fox. 'There's no way across to the Dragon Gardens.'

'I'm cold,' said Mouse.

'Me too,' said Bear. 'And I'm hungry.'

'We'll have to leave the Wilderness,' said Raven. 'I can't see how we can come back again.'

'Never again?' said Mouse.

'It's all flooded,' said Fox. 'It's gone.'

The rain came down harder and felt like needles of ice against Willow's skin. The wind roared through the treetops, and a large branch came crashing down just in front of the Wild Things.

'Uff!' Sniff barked. He began running deeper into the forest.

'We need to follow Sniff!' Willow yelled. 'He'll lead us to shelter.'

The Wild Things followed Sniff along the path, hauling and dragging the tarpaulin full of their belongings. The mud squelched

beneath their feet, and the rain seeped down
their collars and up their sleeves. Even Sniff
trotted along with his ears down and his tail
tucked between his legs.

'Sniff's leading us to the witch's hut,'
shouted Fox.

At first it looked as if the witch was
out. There was a pool of water where the
campfire usually lay, and the door to the hut
was firmly closed. But as they drew near, a
loud 'CAW! CAW! CAW!' came from the
hut and a face appeared at the window.

Lightning flashed, and thunder roared
together.

The door was flung open, and the witch
stood there, her wild yellow hair blowing in
the wind. Not even the witch's crow wanted
to come out into the rain. 'CAW! CAW!' he

31

called from his perch on her shoulder.

'Come in, come in,' said the witch. 'Get out of the storm.'

The Wild Things tumbled through her door into a heap on the floor.

The wind roared like a dragon scrambling over the hut, but it was dry and sheltered inside.

The witch put her hands on her hips. 'What are you doing out here? You look like drowned rats, the lot of you.'

The children had met the witch before. In the world outside the Wilderness, she was a writer. But here they knew her as the witch. She had helped them before, and now they hoped she would help them again.

'River Camp is flooded,' Mouse blurted out. 'We've lost our home.'

The witch leaned closer and poked him with a bony finger. 'You're cold.'

'This is all we have left,' said Fox, pointing to the bulky tarpaulin.

The witch frowned. 'Best shove it in that corner for now. Though I can't say it'll stay dry. The rain is seeping through every hole in the roof.'

There wasn't much room inside, but with the six of them, Sniff, and the witch, it began to warm up. Rain drummed on the tin roof and dripped through leaks into pots and saucepans that the witch had placed around the hut.

'I was just about to make a brew,' said the witch. 'But I haven't got any hot chocolate for you.'

'We've got some,' said Bear. He

rummaged in the tarpaulin and pulled out hot chocolate powder, a biscuit tin, and some mugs. He opened the tin and looked inside. 'Empty,' he sighed. 'At least we have hot chocolate.'

'You all look like you need warming up,' said the witch. She lit a small camping gas stove beneath a pan of water and sat back in a soft armchair. 'Ew!' she said as the chair made a loud squelch. 'It's wetter than a duck's bottom.'

The Wild Things tried to find dry patches on the floor to sit down, and Sniff curled into Willow's lap. They had never been inside the witch's hut before, and Willow couldn't help looking around.

On the table there was a computer, and a large notebook with doodles and scribbled writing on it. The witch had placed an umbrella over her computer to protect it from drips from the roof. There was a small bookcase full of books, their spines furred with damp mould. Each wall of the hut was covered in paintings and drawings of animals and plants.

'Did you do those?' asked Willow.

The witch nodded. 'I like to understand the shape of things. Drawing teaches you how to see.'

'I can't draw,' said Willow.

'Rubbish,' said the witch. 'Everyone can draw.' She gave Willow a stub of pencil and tore a few pieces of paper from a notebook. 'Next time you have a quiet moment, just try it. You don't have to show anyone.'

Willow pushed the pencil and paper into her pocket and looked out at the dark clouds.

'Do you think the rain will ever stop?' asked Mouse.

The witch shrugged her shoulders. 'We need the rain.'

'But it's rained for days,' said Willow. 'Can you put a spell on the rain to make it stop?'

'Suppose it wouldn't start again?' said the witch. 'What then?'

Fox put his head in his hands and sighed. 'It's come at the wrong time. There's a meteor shower in the skies tonight, but it'll be covered in cloud.'

'What's a meteor shower?' asked Mouse.

'Shooting stars,' said Bear.

'Dad was going to let me stay up late and see them,' said Fox.

'I'd love to see shooting stars,' said Raven. 'Imagine if we camped out all night and waited up to see them.'

'You can wish on shooting stars,' said Hare. 'I'd like to see them. I'd make a wish.'

'Well, we can't,' said Fox grumpily. 'We won't be able to see them. It'll be too cloudy. And besides, Nan's telescope has been washed down the river.'

The pan of water began to bubble, and

the witch stood up to pour the boiling water into the mugs. Willow stirred in chocolate powder and handed round the mugs.

Mouse sipped his hot chocolate. 'If I saw a shooting star, I'd wish we could have River Camp back,' he said. 'It was my favourite place in the whole world.'

'I'd wish for a massive chocolate cake,' said Bear. 'I'm starving.'

'I'd wish for an adventure,' said Hare. 'That's the problem with adventures. You never know when they're going to happen.'

Raven stared at the steam rising from her hot chocolate. She wrapped her cloak a little tighter around herself. 'I would wish that I'd never grow up. I want to stay like this now. Forever. Adults forget how to have adventures.'

Hare turned to Willow. 'What would you wish for?'

Willow shrugged her shoulders. But she knew what she'd wish for. She'd wish for Freddie to be well again and not to have to go to hospital. She didn't want to tell everyone her thoughts. 'I wish it'd stop raining,' she said instead.

'Wishes are stupid,' said Fox with a scowl. 'Some wishes can't come true.

Besides, shooting stars aren't stars at all. They're just pieces of space rock that burn up when they come into our atmosphere.' Fox drank the last of his hot chocolate and slammed down his mug. 'I'm going home. There's no point staying. The Wilderness has gone too.'

'Well, I have to go too,' said the witch, standing up. 'I can't work in here today. It's too wet, even for witches. I'll have to come back to dry everything out.'

The witch started packing up her notebook and computer.

'Shh!' said Mouse. 'Do you hear that?'

They all stopped and listened. Something was different. Willow strained her ears to listen.

'I can't hear anything at all,' said Bear.

'Exactly,' said Mouse. 'Willow's wish has already come true, and we haven't even seen a shooting star.'

There was no drumming on the tin roof, no patter through the leaves or drip, drip, drip on to the floor.

The rain had finally stopped.

Chapter 4
Moonrise

They all stepped outside. The ground
steamed. The air was fresh with the smell of
rain on the earth. It was damp, and a thin
mist hung in the air.

'The storm has blown itself out,' said Fox.

'It's going to be a clear night, I think,'
said Hare.

'How can you tell?' asked Willow.

Hare pointed to a plant that curled up
the side of the witch's hut. 'Look at the

glory flowers.'

Most of the bindweed flowers were tightly closed, but some had begun to unfurl, their white petals almost glowing in the dim light.

'They close in the rain,' said Hare, 'and open when good weather is coming.'

The witch nodded. 'It's good to know the wild signs.' She looked up. 'And there,' she said, 'is a patch of blue.'

'Maybe we'll see shooting stars after all,' said Willow.

'I'd love to see them,' said Mouse. 'But I won't be allowed out. I'll have to be in bed.'

'What if we could all camp at my house?' said Raven. 'Willow's staying, so why don't you all come?'

'Camp out all night?' said Mouse. '*All*

night? I've never done that before.'

Raven nodded. 'I'm sure Mum will let us put the tent in the garden.'

'Do you think we'll see shooting stars?' asked Hare.

'I'm sure of it,' said Fox. 'I don't have Nan's telescope, but I'll bring the star map she gave me.'

'A star map?' said Hare wide-eyed. Hare was the map-maker in the Wilderness. 'I've never heard of a star map before. Where does a star map take you?'

Fox smiled. 'Nan said a star map lets you explore the whole universe.'

Willow was surprised that Raven's mum allowed her to have friends over to camp in the garden. Willow's mum and dad usually liked things to be planned ages in advance, but Raven's mum had just said yes.

While the other Wild Things went back to their homes to get permission, sleeping bags, and food for the long night, Willow and Raven helped Raven's mum put up the tent. It was an old canvas tent with heavy poles and a thick groundsheet to keep the inside of the tent dry.

'This was my parents' old tent,' Raven's mum smiled. 'We went everywhere with it. It hasn't been used in years.'

Raven's mum brought some sunloungers and garden chairs from the garden shed and put them in a circle around a firepit. Then she went to find some blankets and sleeping bags inside the house.

Sniff bounded excitedly into the tent.

'Didn't your mum take you camping?'
said Willow.

Raven shrugged her shoulders. 'Mum's
not so keen on camping,' she said. 'Besides,
she works a lot. She doesn't get much time
for a holiday.'

The other Wild Things began to arrive,
dumping their bags inside the tent.

Mouse bounded into the tent with Sniff.
'I've brought a torch so we can explore at
night.'

'I've brought cards,' said Bear. 'It's a
long time to wait until midnight to see the
shooting stars.'

Raven's mum appeared again, with some
barbecue coals. 'I thought you could make
explorer bread,' she said.

'What's explorer bread?' asked Willow.

'I used to make it with friends when I was a child,' said Raven's mum. 'It was the best bread in the world. You'll have to make some later. It's made from flour and water and bicarbonate of soda mixed together to form a dough and then cooked on a stick over the fire.'

The Wild Things spread themselves out in the tent and looked through the opening at the evening sky. The clouds had cleared, and the sky was tinged with pink. The sun was a blazing orange ball as it slipped down behind the trees, casting long shadows across Raven's garden.

Raven sighed. 'It makes me sad seeing the sun go down.'

'Why?' asked Mouse.

'It's a day we can't have again,' said Raven.

The rim of the sun flared as it dipped behind the trees and the air got a little colder. Willow shivered.

'It's weird to think that it's the world turning,' said Fox. 'We're sitting in a tent, in a garden, in a town, in a country, on a round planet spinning round and round in space.'

'Why don't we fly off?' said Mouse. He gripped the edges of the tent, just in case.

'We would if the world stopped,' said Fox. 'The world spins at a thousand miles per hour.'

'How do you know this?' said Hare.

'Nan told me,' said Fox. 'She loved space and things like that. She used to take me stargazing She said she wanted to space travel and dip her toes in the Sea of Tranquillity.'

'Where's that?' said Mouse.

'I'll show you,' said Fox. 'You have to wait for moonrise.'

'Moonrise?' said Mouse.

'Yes,' said Fox. 'No one ever really notices it, but it's my favourite part of the day. Nan used to say moonlight gives us a different way of seeing the world.'

The Wild Things watched the last golden rays of sun turn the western sky from red to orange to pale greenish yellow. Willow tucked her hands into her sleeves as the chill night air crept around them. As the moon rose, it cast a silver light over the rooftops and gardens. It was big and round and bright. The sky became deep indigo, and the world below lost its colours and became shades of blue. Silvery snail trails criss-crossed the wet grass. Diamond beads of dew hung on cobwebs. A bat flitted through the sky chasing a moth, and from inside the Wilderness an owl called into the night.

Willow let her eyes adjust to the darkness and listened out for new sounds. Nightfall revealed a different world that was hidden by day.

Moonrise was magical.

Chapter 5
A Fallen Star

Fox pointed at the moon. 'The Sea of Tranquillity isn't really a sea. It's a crater on the moon.' He pulled a crumpled piece of paper from his pocket and pointed to a map of the moon. 'The shooting stars won't be so bright with a full moon, but we should still see them once the moon has risen. My nan loved the moon. We used to pretend her bed was a rocket ship and visit the moon and all the other planets.'

'My nan said the moon was made of cheese,' said Bear. 'I'm so hungry I could eat the whole of it.'

Raven's stomach rumbled. 'Let's make explorer bread,' she said. She went into the house and brought out a bowl with flour, a small tub of bicarbonate of soda, and a jug of water. Raven's mum came outside to light the coals and find them some old apple tree sticks to toast the wild bread over the fire. She left them a big bowl of jam too.

'How do you make explorer bread?' asked Hare.

Raven shrugged her shoulders. 'I've never made it before. I'm guessing.' She tipped flour into the bowl, sprinkled in some bicarbonate of soda, and poured in some water. Then she worked the mixture into a dough with her hands. She pulled off a piece of gooey dough and speared it on to the end of the stick. The others copied and sat in a circle holding their bread over the glowing embers.

Willow watched the pale wet dough become puffy and golden brown. She smeared it with jam and took a bite. It tasted of the smokiness of the fire and sweetness of jam. It tasted of the cool evening and of the damp earth after the rain. It was the best bread she had ever eaten.

Raven licked jam from her fingers. 'This is why I never want to grow up,' she said. 'Adults never do stuff like this. They just have to work all day, and they're too tired and stressed to have fun.'

The Wild Things played cards by torchlight well into the evening. The night folded around them like a blanket. The moon rose high above them and stars sprinkled across the sky. Raven threw some sticks on the fire, and the shadows danced and leapt around them like forest spirits, just keeping out of reach. It made them all creep nearer to the fire, keeping in the glow of light.

Bear put a pan of water over the hot coals to heat for hot chocolate. Willow fetched a blanket from the tent and wrapped it around her. She stood in the garden and looked up at the stars.

Mouse joined her. 'Where do we look for shooting stars?'

'Towards Cygnus,' said Fox, 'the Swan.'

Mouse stared up at the stars. 'The Swan?'

'Yes,' said Fox. 'Look over to the east, and you see that bright star just over that chimney?'

'Yes,' said Mouse.

'Well, that's Deneb, one of the stars that make up the Swan,' said Fox. 'You can see those stars in a line are the head, neck, and tail, and the two stars that are above and below it make up the wings.'

'What other star patterns are there?' said Mouse.

Fox pointed to the north. 'That's the Pole Star,' he said. 'It's part of the tail of the Little Bear.'

'Little Bear?' said Bear. 'That's me.'

'Is there a hare?' asked Hare.

'No, but there's a lion, and a scorpion, and a big bear,' said Fox.

Willow looked up to the sky and tried to see the swan constellation that Fox had shown them. The more she looked, the more stars she could see.

'When you look at all those stars it makes you feel very small, doesn't it?' said Bear. 'All those billions of stars, and I'm just one person on this planet in the whole of the universe.'

'Maybe there's another planet out there with someone thinking the same thing,' said Hare.

Willow stared up at the stars scattered across the sky. She suddenly felt very alone and very small and very far away from Freddie.

High, high above, a dot of light streaked across the sky.

'There!' cried Willow. 'A shooting star!'

'I saw it,' said Fox.

'Where?' said Raven.

'There! Another one!' said Willow. As they looked, shooting stars trailed across the dark sky.

'Make your wish!' shouted Mouse.

They all craned their necks looking up at Cygnus and the shower of shooting stars that zipped like fireworks high in the sky.

'Oooh,' said Raven, 'there must've been at least ten.'

Willow watched a star streak across the sky. *Make a wish. Make a wish.* Willow wished that Freddie would get better and come home from hospital. The star didn't fade. It got bigger and bigger as it fell towards earth.

Willow gasped as she watched Freddie's star falling through the sky.

It happened so fast. A tumbling glowing ball spinning

down,

down,

down.

It disappeared into the silvery mist over the trees.

A shooting star had fallen into the Wilderness.

Chapter 6
Ghosts and Aliens

'Look!' cried Hare. 'Another one!'

'And another,' said Raven.

The Wild Things watched two more stars falling behind the trees. They seemed to glow bright white by the light of the moon.

Eerie calls echoed into the night from the Wilderness. They were forlorn wailing cries, that seemed to come from another world.

All Willow knew was that Freddie's star was somewhere in the Wilderness and somehow she had to find it.

Mouse held on to Willow's hand. 'What does a fallen star look like?'

Fox turned to the others. 'When meteorites hit the earth they smash into the surface and make big craters. The ground shakes too. They don't wail though.'

'Maybe they're not meteorites,' said Hare.

'What are they then?' asked Raven.

'Aliens,' whispered Bear. 'They've come to earth. I saw a programme about it where a boy was taken up into a spaceship.'

'We didn't see a spaceship,' said Fox.

Mouse tightened his grip of Willow's hand. 'Maybe they're ghosts.'

Hare nodded. 'They were weird, weren't they? They sort of glowed in the moonlight.'

'I counted three of them,' said Willow.

'Three ghosts,' whispered Bear.

'Or vampires,' said Mouse. 'Maybe we'll be sucked into a vampire mist and be turned into vampires too.'

'There's no such thing as ghosts or vampires,' snapped Fox. 'We should go and look.'

'I agree,' said Raven. She pulled on her coat. 'Who's coming?'

Hare hesitated. 'It's a bit late.'

'I don't think I'll be allowed to go into the Wilderness at night,' said Mouse.

'Well, I'm going to look,' said Fox. 'Even if I go by myself.'

'I'll come,' said Raven.

'Me too,' said Willow. She didn't want to say that she had made a wish on that star.

'I'm coming,' said Hare and Bear together.

'I don't want to be left behind,' said Mouse, pulling on another jumper. 'If we get turned into vampires, we'll do it together.'

Fox led the way to the wooden gate at the bottom of the garden. He undid the latch and they all peered out. The Wilderness lay dark and brooding on the other side of the ditch. A lone street lamp lit up the path, circled by a halo of mist.

'It looks spooky,' whispered Mouse.

Wisps of mist crept across from the Wilderness, like fingers blindly reaching to grab passers-by.

Sniff sniffed the air and growled softly.

'What is it, Sniff?' asked Willow.

The eerie cry sounded again, and Sniff whined and put his tail between his legs.

Fox took a step on to the path. 'Come on. Let's go.'

Willow and Raven followed, but Sniff wouldn't budge. He sat down and refused to move.

Something rustled in the Wilderness on the other side of the ditch. The sound was muffled and hidden in the darkness and creeping mist.

Hare hesitated. 'Maybe we should wait,' she said. 'We might get lost in the mist, even with my map.'

'It's dark too,' said Raven. 'If we go, I should tell Mum.'

'It will only get darker and mistier in

there,' said Hare.

'We don't know what's inside,' said Bear.

'Vampires,' whispered Mouse. He crouched down next to Sniff and put his arms around the little dog's neck. 'If Sniff doesn't want to go, then neither do I.'

Hare nodded. 'Mouse is right. My aunt said dogs have a sixth sense for paranormal activity.'

The mist seemed to creep across the bridge, swirling on to the path as if something was coming over from the Wilderness. Thin wispy tendrils reached out for them, glowing in the moonlight. The eerie call came again.

The mist reached Fox, and he shivered. It curled around Raven and Willow too, and Willow could feel its damp, clammy grasp.

'The vampires are coming,' said Mouse.

'I think we should go back,' whispered Raven.

'I'm not scared,' said Fox.

'Me neither,' said Willow. But she felt uneasy. Sniff didn't want to go into the Wilderness. Maybe Freddie's star would have to wait.

Mouse started backing away into the safety of Raven's garden.

They all followed, and Raven shut the gate, putting the latch down firmly, but the vampire mist slid underneath and seeped through the gaps in the hedge. It reached out for them.

'Into the tent!' cried Raven.

They all piled into the tent, zipped the flysheet and inner lining shut, and crawled into their sleeping bags, and under duvets. Sniff crept in between Willow and Mouse and put his head in his paws.

'Can vampires open tents?' whispered Mouse.

'Aliens might just suck up our tent with us in it,' said Bear.

'I think we investigate at first light,' said Raven.

'I agree,' said Fox.

'Unless we've been taken into space by then,' said Bear.

'Or turned into vampires,' said Mouse.

Willow curled deeper under her duvet. She wasn't sure she believed in vampires and aliens, but somehow the dark and the mist made everything seem terrifying and possible.

'Let's sleep,' said Hare, 'so we can get up first thing.'

'I don't think I can sleep,' said Mouse, pressing himself closer to Willow and Sniff. 'I don't think I'll ever sleep again.'

But they did sleep. One by one, they drifted into their dreams. Only Sniff kept one ear awake for vampires, ghosts, and aliens, and any other dangers that might come their way.

Chapter 7
Cygnus Cygnus

Willow woke first with Sniff licking her face, telling her it was time to get up.

She unzipped the tent and peered out. The air smelled damp and cool, and the world was shrouded in whiteness. The mist was so thick that she couldn't see the end of the garden. She couldn't help thinking about the fallen star and the wish she had made last night. What if they were connected? Maybe by finding the star she could somehow help Freddie. She had to find Freddie's star.

'What time is it?' asked Raven, yawning and rubbing her eyes.

Fox rolled over and looked at his watch. 'Seven o'clock.'

'We slept through sunrise,' said Raven.

'There's no sun to see,' said Willow. 'Just thick fog.'

Mouse woke up with a sharp intake of breath and ran his fingers along his teeth. 'I'm not a vampire,' he said, relieved.

Bear peered out of the tent. 'Maybe we're in a spaceship and that's why we can't see anything out there.'

Fox sat up. 'It's fog, that's all. We need to go to the Wilderness and find the fallen stars.'

75

Raven stretched and crawled out of the tent. 'I'll go and tell Mum we're going and get some breakfast too,' she said.

Shortly after, she came back down the garden with an armful of bread rolls and began shovelling them into the big pockets of her coat. 'Let's go.'

The Wild Things left the safety of the garden and trotted down the path. The Wilderness was shrouded in mist, but it didn't seem as scary as the night before. Raven led the way over the plank of wood across the Green Slime River into the Wilderness.

They all stood still, listening in the strange white silence.

'We might get lost,' said Mouse.

'I've got the map,' said Hare.

They crawled through the tunnel of brambles and thorns, the secret entrance to the Wilderness. They stood up and brushed the mud from their knees at the top of the hill above the place where River Camp had once been.

'It's too foggy to see down into the valley,' said Bear.

'I'm glad,' said Mouse. 'I don't want to see our valley flooded. I want to remember it how it was.'

'Me too,' said Fox.

'How do we know where to look for the fallen stars?' said Willow.

The eerie cry they had heard the night before sounded again from the direction of the swamp. It was a forlorn, sad cry, joined by two others. Sniff growled and set off along the ridge.

A path led them down
to the edge of the flooded
swamp. The water stretched
out before them into the
veil of whiteness. It was
like a vast endless lake.
Willow found it hard
to tell how far they had
travelled as everything
seemed further in the mist.

Sniff growled again.

'Look there,' said Willow. 'There's something moving on the water.'

Something emerged from the silvery mist. It glided silently towards them across the water. It seemed to glow brighter than the mist.

'A swan,' whispered Willow. 'It's the fallen star.'

'Of course!' said Hare. 'That makes sense. It fell out of the constellation of Cygnus.'

They watched the swan slide between the flooded trees, ripples of water spreading out behind it. It circled then swam further along the lake edge, stopping to look at them.

'It wants us to follow it,' whispered Willow.

The Wild Things paddled along the lake edge, their feet sinking into the sticky mud, until they clambered over a fallen tree trunk to see another swan in the water. It flapped its wings and honked at them.

'You have to watch swans,' said Bear. 'They can break your arm.'

'That's not true,' said Hare.

'Still,' said Fox. 'I wouldn't want to argue with them.'

Sniff was barking at something, but he
wasn't barking at the swans in the water.
There was another swan lying on the
muddy bank. It was a pale grey colour, and
its long neck was folded back under its
wing. The two white swans waddled on to
the mud, hissing at Sniff and flapping their
wings at him, but the grey swan didn't seem
to notice. It tucked its head further into its
feathers and didn't move at all.

'That grey one doesn't look very well,'
said Willow. 'Maybe it's sick or injured.

Maybe that's why it fell out of the sky.'

'I think that's a young one,' said Hare.

Willow thought of the shooting star and the wish she had made. Her wish had fallen to earth and now she had to save it. She thought of the grey swan, and she thought of Freddie. This was Freddie's star. She was sure of it. She felt an ache deep in her chest. She hadn't heard from Mum and Dad, and her phone had lost battery power. Freddie and this swan were all mixed up in her mind. She felt helpless that she hadn't been able to go to the hospital with Freddie.

The star she had wished on had fallen out of the sky.

Maybe if she could somehow save this swan, she might be able to help Freddie too.

Chapter 8
Swan Whisperer

'There's something wrong with it,' said Willow. 'We have to help it.'

Bear sat down and rubbed his belly. 'Perhaps it's hungry and tired. I don't think I can go on until I have breakfast.'

Raven pulled some bread rolls from her pockets. 'Maybe it wants bread.'

'Bread isn't good for swans,' said Fox.

'It's better than nothing if it hasn't had any food,' said Raven.

Raven took a bread roll and started to walk towards the swans, but the white swans honked and flapped back into the water. The grey swan lurched to its feet and followed behind the others. It swam away into the flooded swamp and tucked its head back underneath its wing.

The fog hung low over the flooded swamp, and it was difficult to tell where the water ended and where the sky began.

'Let's leave the bread for them,' said Raven.

'We need to stay with it and make sure it eats,' said Willow.

'It's not going to come close if we're here,' said Hare.

'Let's build a bird hide,' said Willow. 'Then we can watch it from there.'

The Wild Things gathered branches to make a small den and camouflaged it with leaves. Bear and Mouse found a large log and dragged it inside to make a dry seat, and they left a small spy hole between twigs to peer through.

Willow scattered pieces of bread along

the muddy bank, and they all bundled
into the bird hide and waited. The swans
watched them from the safety of the water,
but they didn't come near.

The Wild Things watched and waited.

And waited.

And waited.

'I'm bored,' whispered Mouse.

'I'm hungry,' whispered Bear.

'Shh!' said Willow. 'The swans can hear
us. They won't come if they hear us.'

Hare tapped her feet impatiently. 'I'm
hungry too.'

'Me too,' said Raven. 'We'll go home for
lunch and check on the swans later.'

'But we need to stay and make sure the
grey one is OK,' said Willow.

'There's not much more we can do,' said

Fox.

Willow felt hot tears burn in her eyes. She turned away from them all and stared out at the swans. 'Well, I'm staying,' she said. 'I'm not leaving.'

Raven pulled the last bread roll from her pocket. 'You can give them this too. We'll bring some more food when we come back.'

Mouse stopped outside. 'Do you want me to stay with you?'

'I'm fine,' snapped Willow. She felt cross with them all. She was annoyed that they were bored and hungry and didn't want to help. And she felt cross at Fox for saying there was nothing they could do. Willow watched the Wild Things leave the bird hide and disappear into the mist, then she hugged Sniff against her chest and stared out at the grey swan floating on the water. 'I won't leave you,' she promised.

Willow scattered some more bread at the waters edge and crept back inside the bird hide. She sat in silence, listening to the distant hum of traffic. Here, in the bird hide, it was quiet and peaceful. The air smelled damp and earthy after the rain. She sat so still that she felt as if she was becoming part of the Wilderness. Small birds flitted down to peck at the breadcrumbs. Weak sunlight tried to pierce the mist. Willow started to notice tiny details: the heart-shaped leaves of ivy, the silver ripples on the water's edge, and birdsong falling from the treetops. Willow took the notebook and pencil stub from her coat pocket and began to draw. She drew the swans and their reflections. She shaded the dark mud and the long shadows of the tree trunks. The witch had been right. By trying to draw, she was learning to see. It wasn't a bad drawing either, she thought. Slowly, the two adult swans glided nearer. They waddled out on to the muddy bank and began to feed on bread, picking up pieces with their beaks and guzzling them down.

The grey swan swam closer too. It paddled up on to the mud and sank down on to its belly. It tried to peck at the bread but didn't seem able to pick any up. It lay its long neck on the ground and closed its eyes. It was only then that Willow noticed there was something different about this swan. There was something around its beak.

'Stay there, Sniff,' Willow whispered.

Sniff lay down and whined but didn't move. Willow wasn't sure if it was true that swans could break an arm, or if the two adult swans would chase her, but she had to try to help the grey swan. She crept closer and closer to it. The two adult swans waddled into the water and honked at her, ruffling their feathers indignantly.

Willow tried to ignore them and crawled up to the grey swan. It just lay watching her. Now she could see a small piece of clear plastic, small and thin enough to be almost invisible, but strong enough to keep the swan's beak tightly closed. She thought the swan might try to struggle and flap away, but it stayed still, watching her. Maybe it was too weak to move, or maybe it knew she was trying to help. Willow crouched

next to it and gently lifted the swan's head on to her lap. The piece of plastic looked like it had once been a ring from an old bottle top. Willow gently eased it off the grey swan's beak. It shook its head, suddenly realizing it was free of the plastic and could open its beak again. Willow held some crumbled bread roll in her hand and watched as the swan gobbled it down.

'You were just tired and hungry,' said Willow, reaching in her pocket for another roll. She tore it into pieces, held them on her upturned palm, and watched the swan eat them from her hand. Willow wondered how long it had not been able to eat.

Willow tore up the last bread roll and watched while the swan ate the lot.

'Uff, uff, uff,' barked Sniff.

Willow turned to see Sniff standing outside the bird hide, barking at the mist. The Wild Things slowly emerged, and the grey swan beat its wings in Willow's face and launched itself into the water. The other swans swam over to it, waggling their tails.

Hare ran over to her. 'Are you OK?'

'You're a swan whisperer,' said Raven. 'How did it let you get so close?'

'It had plastic around its beak,' said Willow, holding up the plastic ring. 'That's why it couldn't eat.'

Fox took the piece of plastic in his hand and turned it over. 'You saved the swan, Willow. It would have died if you hadn't taken this off.'

Bear stared after the swans. 'There must be other animals that don't get helped.'

'Do you think the swan will be OK?' asked Mouse.

'I think it needs more food,' said Willow. 'It must be starving.'

Hare reached into her bag. 'We've brought some more rolls, and some lunch for you,' she said.

Willow broke up the bread and scattered it at the water's edge. 'They won't come if we're all here,' she said.

'We'll come back later,' said Raven.

Willow nodded. The swan could feed by itself now. It probably needed rest too.

A weak sun glowed yellow in the sky, and the mist began to lift. Raven led the way along the ridge but stopped so suddenly that the Wild Things bumped into each other.

'Look,' said Raven, pointing below them.

Willow and the Wild Things looked down into the valley at the bend in the river where River Camp had once been. The mist had lifted, showing that the floodwaters had receded. But there was no trace of River Camp. Everything had been washed away.

River Camp had gone.

Chapter 9
River Camp Again

The Wild Things clambered down to the valley in stunned silence. The place where River Camp had once been was just a patch of muddy grass. Even the stones around the campfire had been washed away.

Hare sat down and stared at the mess. 'I'm glad I got my map in time.'

'I wish I'd got my nan's telescope,' said Fox. 'It'll be washed away by now.'

Bear was wandering up and down the river's edge. 'The suitcase is here!' he yelled.

The Wild Things ran over and looked down into the river. Fallen branches had piled up together, forming a small dam. In the middle of the dam was the old leather suitcase.

Bear waded in and hauled out some of the branches so that they could reach the suitcase.

Fox grasped it and pulled it to the side. He opened it up and pulled out a small rectangular case. Inside the case, a small brass telescope lay on a bed of soggy blue velvet. He pulled it out and held one end to his eye. 'It's a bit wet inside,' he said. 'But it'll dry.'

'Look,' said Bear. 'These branches

must've come down in the storm. There are loads of them. We can build a new den with them.'

Raven hauled another branch out of the river. 'We're going to make River Camp again,' she said. 'Only this time it's going to be bigger and better.'

Fox and Raven leaned a long sturdy branch against the large oak to make a frame, and they gathered more smaller branches to lay against it.

Mouse and Hare went into the Forest of Forever Night to find fir tree branches to use as roof covering for the shelter. Bear and Willow went in search of stones to make a ring around a new campfire, and they found some logs to use as stools to sit on.

'If only we had dry wood to make a fire,' said

Bear. 'We'll have to make a new log store now.'

They worked all day remaking River Camp from the muddy waste.

They hardly noticed the sun passing overhead and sinking down behind the trees.

Willow's arms and legs ached, and she was covered in mud. Thick clogs of mud hung from Sniff's fur too. The sun had dried the ground, and the Wild Things lay down, exhausted.

'Uff,' barked Sniff. Only Sniff had noticed the figure on the hill above. He barked and ran up to meet the witch, who was on her way down, carrying their tarpaulin of blankets and cushions. She was wearing a rucksack too.

'I thought you'd need dry firewood,' the witch said.

She dropped the rucksack next to their campfire and pulled out dry logs and kindling. 'I've brought fresh water too, to make hot chocolate.'

Hare set about lighting the fire. The dry kindling spat and fizzled and caught, the flames licking around the logs. Wood smoke drifted into the air.

'It's a proper camp again,' said Raven.

The Wild Things all crowded nearer to the fire to warm their hands.

'I'm hungry,' said Mouse.

The witch reached into her rucksack again and pulled out a tin. 'Chocolate cake,' she said. 'I made it yesterday when it was raining. Who wants some?'

'Wishes do come true,' said Bear. 'I wished on the shooting star for chocolate cake.'

The witch chuckled. 'And I heard that wish. Chocolate cake is my favourite too.'

'And I wished that River Camp would be saved,' said Mouse. 'Maybe wishing on a star does work.'

Raven shrugged. 'I wished never to grow up,' she said. She stared into the fire. 'I don't want to be an adult. Ever. Adults can't see the magic in places like this. Maybe that'll happen to me, and it'll happen so slowly that I won't even notice. And I'll think you're silly and boring, but really I'll be the boring one, and I'll never want to go on an adventure again.'

The witch smiled. 'None of us can stop growing older,' she said. 'But if you stay

curious about the world, it doesn't matter what age
you are when an adventure comes calling.'

'I'm going to go on adventures when I'm older,' said Hare. 'I'm going to travel by starlight across the oceans.' She pulled out a piece of paper and showed a map of the sky. 'This is thanks to Fox for teaching me about the stars.'

The witch stoked the fire. 'Yes,' she said. 'And when you are old like me and sleeping under the stars on your boat on the ocean, you will remember this place as your first adventure.'

Bear wiped the cake crumbs from his mouth. 'Maybe that's what wishes are. They don't just happen. They are things you dream about that you have to help make come true.'

Fox folded his arms and stared into the fire. 'Not all wishes can come true. I want my nan to be here. She wanted to see shooting stars with me.'

The witch poured boiling water into cups and stirred in the hot chocolate powder. 'Your nan taught you all about the moon and stars, and you've shared that with us. People live on within us and shine like stars and guide us.'

Fox held the telescope in his hands and smiled. 'Nan would have loved it here.'

Willow stared into the flames. She thought about her wish, about Freddie. She thought about the swan too. She had tried to help it. She couldn't fly for it, but she had done everything she could. Maybe that's how Mum and Dad felt. Maybe they were just doing the best they could too.

The sun sank lower in the sky.

'I can't believe we've been out all day,' said Hare. 'We'd better get back.'

'There's somewhere I need to go first,' said Willow. 'I need to see the swan.'

Chapter 10
Feather Fall

The water levels had already fallen by the time the Wild Things reached the swamp. Small islands of tufty grass dotted the surface of the water. But as much as Willow looked, she couldn't see the swans at all. The sky had turned pink with the setting sun.

'Maybe they've gone,' she said. She tossed some bread at the water's edge, and a splashing and honking came from the other side as the grey swan and two adults flapped across the water towards them.

'The grey swan can't fly,' said Hare.

It dabbled for bread while the adult swans kept their distance. They looked restless, shaking their heads and looking up at the sky.

'Shh!' said Mouse. 'What's that?'

There was a whistling sound and beating of wings from high above. A flock of swans in the shape of a big letter V passed overhead.

'Honk! Honk! Honk!' they called.

The adult swans called back and began to flap their wings, their feet slapping against the water surface as they ran, gaining speed. They rose up into the air, above the treetops and circled above, calling to the grey swan.

The Wild Things watched the grey swan spread its wings wide. Then it turned and faced the long expanse of water. It began to beat its wings.

Willow held her breath. She hoped it was strong enough now. *Please fly, please fly.*

It used the water as a runway, flapping speedily along until it was clear of the flooded swamp. Then it folded its feet up gracefully underneath its body, like the wheels of a plane. It rose up and skimmed the tops of the trees and flew in a wide circle before joining the other swans. The Wild Things watched the three of them join the end of the line of birds.

'Wooohooo!' cheered Bear.

Willow squinted into the sun and watched the swans disappear. She wished Freddie could have seen the swans too. She wanted to tell him all about them.

High in the sky, something caught the light. A lone pale grey feather spiralled downwards towards her. Willow caught it in her hand. It was so light, it hardly weighed a

thing. But it was a gift
from the swan, thought Willow.
A gift to give Freddie, to help him to fly.

The Wild Things crawled back through the
Holloway and walked in silence across the
Green Slime River. It seemed strange being
out of the Wilderness. Everything seemed
smaller, less magical, somehow. Willow
noticed the Wild Things become less wild.
They looked more human now.

Raven's mum was waiting for them in
the garden. 'Where've you been? I was just
coming to look for you,' she said. 'You've
been gone all day.'

'We were just playing,' said Raven.

Raven's mum laughed. 'I think you'll all
need a bath when you get home.' She turned

to Willow. 'Your mum left a message to say she's home.'

'How's Freddie?' asked Willow.

'She didn't say,' said Raven's mum.

Willow shoved her belongings into her bag and thanked Raven and her mum for having her. Then she ran home along the path behind the gardens, her heart beating fast. Was Freddie still in hospital? Sniff ran ahead of her. He scrambled through the hole in the hedge.

'Uff, uff!' barked Sniff.

Willow followed him to see Freddie playing in the garden, splashing in a big puddle in welly boots.

'Freddie!' she yelled.

Freddie ran to her, and she hauled him up in her arms.

'Are you feeling better?' asked Willow.

Freddie nodded. He put his arms around her neck. 'Story?' he asked.

Willow smiled. She carried him over to the garden bench and sat him down. 'I did promise to find a story,' she said. 'And I found one. It's about a shooting star.' She pulled out the long swan feather and her drawing of the three swans.

Freddie held the feather in his hands and climbed on to her lap to listen. He looked at the picture of the three swans on the flooded swamp.

Willow held him tight, thinking of her adventure with the Wild Things in the Wilderness. 'Are you ready?' she asked.

Freddie leaned into her, his head against her chest, waiting for the story. Sniff curled up beside them.

Willow smiled and began. 'It had rained for days. Rained and rained and rained. It hadn't stopped . . .'

How to make your own explorer bread!

You can make your own explorer bread, just like the Wild Things. This recipe is really easy, and perfect for cooking outdoors over a campfire.

Ingredients

500g self-raising flour

300 to 500ml water

A pinch of salt

A pinch of bicarbonate of soda

Jam

1. Before you head out to your camp or den, put your flour, salt, and bicarbonate of soda in an airtight container.

2. Now, gradually add water and mix everything together with a spoon.

3. On a clean surface, knead the dough by moulding it into a ball, pressing it down, and then reshaping it.

4. Roll the dough into a long sausage shape.

5. Find a good, clean, stick and wind your dough around it.

6. Put your stick over the fire to cook, turning occasionally. You should be able to see it puff up a little and turn golden brown as it cooks.

7. After just a few minutes, your dough will have turned into delicious bread.

8. Add jam and enjoy!

Gill Lewis spent much of her childhood in the garden, where she ran a small zoo and a veterinary hospital for creepy-crawlies, mice, and birds. When she grew up she became a real vet and travelled from the Arctic to Africa in search of interesting animals and places.

Gill now writes books for children. Her previous novels have published to worldwide critical acclaim and have been translated into more than twenty languages.

She lives in the depths of Somerset with her husband and three children and writes from a tree house in the company of squirrels.

Rebecca Bagley is a children's book illustrator in the south-west of England.

Illustrators are a funny sort of grown-up. They do grown-up things, like brushing their teeth (every day), but they also sit around drawing pictures and then call it a job. Recently, Rebecca has been drawing a lot of leaves, as well as all the magical things that live amongst them, and she couldn't be happier about it.

In between drawings, Rebecca daydreams about having her own garden one day, where she will grow tomatoes, practise handstands, and have a really big dog. Until then, she entertains herself and her little family by feeding new and weird flavours to her baby girl who, so far, has been a very good sport.

Ready for more great stories?
Try one of these...

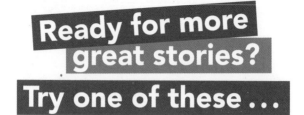